W9-DET-237

30036000060887

MAY 2 4 2001

Princess Josie's Pets

by Maryann Macdonald

Illustrated by
Diana Cain Bluthenthal

Hyperion Books for Children
New York

For Barbara Lucas,
with affection and admiration
—M. M.

For my two Prince Charmings,
Vince and Cameron,
and every animal they know and love
—D. C. B.

Text © 1998 by Maryann Macdonald.
Illustrations © 1998 by Diana Cain Bluthenthal.

Printed in the United States of America.

First Edition

1 3 5 7 9 10 8 6 4 2

The artwork for each picture is prepared using pen and ink.
This book is set in 16-point Berkeley Book.

Library of Congress Cataloging-in-Publication Data
Macdonald, Maryann.
Princess Josie's pets / Maryann Macdonald ; illustrated by Diana Cain Bluthenthal. —1st ed.
p.   cm.
Summary: Princess Josie wants a puppy for her eighth birthday, but first she must prove to the King and Queen that she can be responsible for its care.
ISBN 0-7868-1134-X (pbk.)—ISBN 0-7868-2263-5 (lib. bdg.)
[1. Princesses—Fiction. 2. Animals—Fiction. 3. Pets—Fiction.]
I. Bluthenthal, Diana Cain, ill. II. Title.
PZ7.M1486Pr   1997
[E]—dc20   96-27186

Contents

1

Pet Problems

"It's not fair!" said Princess Josie. She punched the pink silk pillow on her canopy bed. "No way is it fair."

"Hmmph!" said Nanny Mulligan. "Just look who's talking about fair. Luckiest little girl in all the world."

Princess Josie pulled the pillow over her head. She didn't want to hear any more.

Just because she lived in a palace . . . and her bedroom was in the tower . . . and she had forty-two party dresses . . . just because of a few things like that everyone thought she was lucky. But she didn't have the only thing she really wanted—a dog.

"I love dogs more than anything in the whole world!" she had told her family at breakfast.

They all sat in the royal dining room. Around them hung huge paintings of past royal families. Lots of *them* had dogs.

Queen Cristobel buttered her toast neatly. She spread it with honey, just to the edges. Then she put down her silver knife on the edge of her gold-rimmed plate.

"Last year you loved gerbils more than anything in the whole world," she said.

Josie sighed. She wished the queen would forget about Tristan and Isolde. But the queen never forgot.

"I did love my gerbils," said Josie.

"Then you should have looked after them," said Queen Cristobel. She took a sip of her tea.

"I tried to!" said Josie.

She had just let Tristan out of his cage for a minute. To play.

But then Isolde snuck out, too. They hid behind the walls. They started having babies. Hundreds of them.

King Maximillian wiped his thick mustache with his napkin.

"Our palace was overrun with gerbils!" he said. "And then there was that goose. . . ."

"Gander," Josie corrected him.

Josie had found Edwin freezing in his nest. His wing was hurt and he couldn't fly.

"I took good care of him," said Josie.

"Indeed," said the king. He helped himself to more bacon. "You slept with him in your bedroom. You swam with him in the palace pool. But then you let him go!"

"I had to," said Josie.

Didn't King Max know how sad she was to set Edwin free?

"He was wild," Josie explained. "Dogs are not. They are *meant* to be pets! Like horses. And you let Ozzie have a horse!"

"Osbert is ten," said Queen Cristobel, "and very mature for his age."

Prince Osbert smiled. Then he sliced the top off his egg. He did it very neatly. Just like his mother.

Josie kicked him under the table.

Queen Cristobel folded her napkin and stood up.

"By the time you're ten, Josephina," she

said, "I'm sure you'll be ready to take care of a dog."

TEN? How could Josie wait two whole years? More than two years of dull, dogless days! It was more than she could stand.

Josie took the pillow off her head. Today was over. She needed a plan for tomorrow.

"What am I going to do, Nanny?" she said.

"Say a little prayer, love," Nanny said. "That's what I would do."

Prayer, thought Josie. What good would that do? All last week she had prayed for Elvis to come back. She wanted him to sing at her eighth birthday party in June. So far there was no sign of him.

But Josie knelt down beside her bed anyway.

"Dear God," she said. "Please help me get a dog for my birthday. It doesn't matter if Elvis can't come to my party. Just help me prove I am old enough to take care of a dog.

"Amen."

"Very nice, love," said Nanny Mulligan.

She tucked Josie under the soft velvet comforter. Then she turned out the light and tiptoed out the door.

When the light went out, Josie felt as black as the tower room. She would *never* get a dog. She just knew it. Not until she was TEN YEARS OLD! Then, suddenly, she had an idea.

"God helps those who help themselves," Nanny Mulligan always said. So Josie would help herself.

She smiled. She snuggled down in the pink velvet. And she fell into a deep sleep. In her dream, she saw her own painting hanging in the royal dining room. And standing right beside her was a happy golden dog.

2

The Boring Book

The lady behind the library desk wore half glasses. She looked up at Princess Josie over the top of them.

"Isn't this your mother's library card?" she asked.

Josie shifted from one foot to the other. "Mine was in my pocket," she said. "It went through the wash."

The librarian frowned. "Does your

mother know you have hers?"

"Um . . . no," said Josie. She had not told Queen Cristobel about her own library card. "But she won't mind. I know she won't. She never uses her card anyway. All she reads is *Kingdoms Today*. And we have a prescription for that."

"You mean a *subscription* to that," said the librarian.

"It comes in the mail," said Josie. "Anyway, Mother likes me to read. Really she does."

"Queen Cristobel does like to see the princess with a book," said Josie's driver, John, helpfully.

"Well . . . ," said the librarian, "all right. But just one book today."

Josie looked at the stack of dog books

she had picked out. She took the biggest, fattest one.

"Here," she said.

The librarian took the card out and stamped it. Then she zapped the book through a machine.

"This will be due in three weeks' time," she said. Then, without looking up again, she went back to her files.

Josie hugged *Care of Canine Companions*. It had 736 pages. It was heavy.

"I'll carry that for you, missy," said John.

But Josie said no. She was going to prove that she could do everything she had to do to look after her dog—even carry her dog book.

On the way home in her limo, Josie read the chapter called "House Training."

During lunch in the kitchen with Cook, she read "Feeding Requirements." In the apple orchard after lunch, she read "Diseases and Parasites."

Care of Canine Companions was a hard book, full of big words. It was a boring book, full of dull advice. But worst of all, it was a sickening book, full of awful pictures. When Josie saw the ones of ringworms and roundworms, she wasn't sure she wanted a dog after all.

Where were the king and queen

anyway? Here she was, reading this awful book, and they didn't even know!

"The queen's in meetings today," said Nanny, "and the king's gone shopping. They won't be back till after tea."

After tea!

Josie decided to read later. But who was there to play with? Not Perfect Prince Osbert. He was out riding his stupid horse. Josie hoped he would fall off and break his perfect neck. She went to find Daniel, the stableboy.

All afternoon Daniel and Josie jumped off a rope into a big haystack. Frakin, the stableman, was out. But at half past six, he came back.

"Off with you!" he yelled at Josie. "And you," he said to Daniel, "back to work!"

Josie ran back to the palace as fast as she could go. Her heart was pounding. She was scared of Frakin. He never smiled or laughed. He scowled and shouted.

"Wherever were you?" asked Nanny when Josie got back. "It's been raining cats and dogs!"

Raining cats and dogs! Josie pulled a piece of sweet hay from her hair and chewed on it. She liked to think of cats and dogs falling from the sky.

Little kittens with parachutes. Little puppies in the petunias. You could pick one up and keep it. Instead of having to read a stupid book . . .

Oh no! Josie thought. The book! She had left it in the apple orchard—in the rain!

3

In Trouble Again

*C*are of Canine Companions was wrecked. It was soaked. The ink was blurred. But maybe if Josie dried it out and ironed the pages flat . . .

Josie took the book to the palace laundry room. No one was there.

Josie opened the dryer and put the book in. She set the dryer on high. Now *Care of Canine Companions* would get good and dry.

Care of Canine Companions did get good and dry. It also fell apart. The cover came off. All 736 pages fell out. It was no use ironing them now.

The librarian would tell Mother. Mother would think Josie was careless. And she would never, ever let her have a dog . . .

unless Josie could pay for the book. Then Mother would never know.

Queen Cristobel gave Josie money when she needed it. But Josie had to tell her what it was for. This time she could not tell her.

I'll have to get the money myself, thought Josie. But how?

Josie went to Cook.

"If I help you bake, will you pay me?" she asked.

Cook laughed. "Pay you to get in my way?" Cook asked. "Not likely."

Josie went to John, her driver.

"If I help you wash cars, will you pay me?" she asked.

John scratched his head. "What will the queen say if I let you do my work?" he asked.

So Josie went to Nanny.

"If I help you sew, will you pay me?"

"If you want something done well," said Nanny, "do it yourself. That's what I always say."

No one wanted to pay the princess. She

walked sadly to the stable. She found Daniel.

"I came to say good-bye," she said. "I'm running away."

Josie told him why. "I'll never get a dog now," she said. "So I'm leaving."

Daniel nodded. He understood. "I *love* my cat Smoky," he said.

Josie was jealous. "Where is that fat old thing?" she asked.

"Smoky's not fat!" said Daniel.

"She was last time I saw her," said Josie.

"Well, she's not anymore," whispered Daniel. "Her kittens are ten days old!"

"Kittens!" said Josie. "You never told me!"

Daniel clapped his hand over Josie's mouth. "I couldn't," he said. "I couldn't tell anyone. If Frakin found out, he'd drown 'em."

"Drown them?" said Josie, horrified.

"That's right," said Daniel. "He'd drown 'em soon as look at 'em. So I got to keep 'em secret. Until they're old enough to give away."

"Can I see them, Daniel?" the princess begged. "Please?"

Daniel shook his head. "Not yet," he said. "They're too little to play with."

"Well," said the princess, "when *can* I play with them?"

"When their eyes open," said Daniel.

"When will that be?" asked Josie.

"Any day now," said Daniel.

Well, thought Josie. Maybe she would stay after all. Just until the kittens' eyes

opened. The library book wasn't due yet.
Not for three more weeks. She didn't have
to run away until then.

4
Kittens!

"*P*ing!"

Josie's eyes popped open.

"*Ping!*"

What was that sound?

"*Ping!*"

It came from the tower window. She climbed out of bed and looked out.

There was Daniel. Josie opened the window.

"The kittens!" he said. "Their eyes are open! Come and see."

Josie pulled on her jeans over her pajama bottoms. She put on her sneakers without any socks. She grabbed a sweater, slid down three flights of stairs, and was out the heavy oak door before you could say Abyssinian.

"Where are they?" she asked Daniel.

"Follow me," he said.

They tramped across the mushy ground. They came to a small shed.

Daniel opened the door. There was Smoky, lying in a blanket. Four tiny kittens lay beside her. Smoky was licking them gently.

"Oh," said Josie softly.

She had never seen such new kittens.

There was a fluffy white one. There was a pretty striped one. There was a fat yellow one. And there was a skinny black one with a crooked tail.

Josie loved them all.

"Oh," she said again. "What are their names?"

"The white one's Snowy," said Daniel. "And the yellow one's Buttercup. The striped one's Tweedy 'cause he looks like he's wearin' a suit."

"What about the black one?" said Josie.

"He hasn't got a name yet," said Daniel. "I was thinkin' 'bout Ratty."

"That's an awful name!" said the princess.

But the black kitten did look like a rat. Even his tiny crooked tail was skinny, just like a rat's.

Snowy, Buttercup, and Tweedy pushed up to Smoky. They were hungry for milk.

The black kitten tried to push up, too. But the others batted him away.

"He only gets what's left over," said Daniel. "That's why he's so skinny."

"It's not fair!" said Josie. She picked up the black kitten. She set him on her hand.

"*Pe-weep!*" he cried.

Josie petted his head with one finger.

"Don't cry, baby," she said. "I'll fatten you up. I promise."

5

Homes for the Homeless

Two and a half weeks later, the black kitten lay in Josie's arms. He had just drunk three doll bottles full of canned milk. Josie rocked him.

"You ain't nothin' but a hound cat," she sang, "out cryin' all the time."

The kitten gazed up at Josie adoringly. "*Maow*," he sang back. "*Me-wow maow*."

"Did you hear that?" Josie said to Daniel. "Elvis can sing!"

"You feed him too much," said Daniel. "He's getting fat."

Josie smiled. It was true. Elvis loved to eat. He was making up for lost time.

"He'll slim down," said Josie, "once we let him out of this shed to run around."

"Josie," said Daniel, "we can't ever let Elvis out of this shed. He's got to stay in here until we give him away. Him and the others, too. They're almost four weeks old now."

"Kittens stay with their mother until they're six weeks old," said Josie. "That's what Nanny told me."

"Not these kittens," said Daniel. "They're gettin' too big. And too noisy. Frakin will find 'em."

He sighed. "They've got all their teeth now," he said. "They've got to go."

Sunbeams slipped through the cracks in the wall of the shed. Snowy and Buttercup and Tweedy tried to catch them. Snowy bumped heads with Buttercup and blinked her blue eyes in surprise. Buttercup shook herself. Her fur stood out like duck down.

"Daniel," said Josie, "these kittens are so pretty we won't have to give them away. We can sell them!"

Daniel stroked Smoky from her shoulders to the tip of her bushy tail.

"Think so?" he said.

"Sure," said the princess. "We'll put up a sign on the back gate.

"We might even make enough money to pay for that awful library book!"

So first thing next morning, Josie and Daniel made their sign. Then they carried the kitten basket to the back gate of the palace and put up the sign.

Lots of people stopped. Lots of people smiled. Lots of people played with the kittens. And one lady in a blue hat paid five silver shillings for Snowy. But no one else wanted to buy a kitten.

"I can't understand it," said Josie as she and Daniel lugged the basket back to the shed. "Why doesn't anyone want them?"

"Maybe John will take one," Daniel said.

But John said no.

"Tweedy's a handsome fellow," said John, "but I don't think I should take him. I'm out driving so much."

But Tweedy knew what to do. He

jumped up onto John's shoulder. He licked John's ear.

John took off his cap and scratched his head.

"I guess he could always go with me," he said.

Tweedy had found a home.

"Maybe Cook will take one, too," Josie said.

"A kitten?" said Cook. "To leave footprints on my clean table? No thank you."

But Buttercup knew what to do, too. She rubbed her soft little body against Cook's large ankle.

"*Meow*," she said politely.

She cocked her head and looked up at Cook with her big green eyes. Cook poured some cream into a saucer.

"Cats do keep mice away," he said, "and they're such clean animals."

Buttercup had found a home.

Now only Elvis was left.

"Maybe Nanny will take him," said Daniel.

"Elvis is not Nanny's type," said Josie. She watched him stalk a butterfly.

He pounced. He missed. The butterfly fluttered away.

"I'll just have to take Elvis with me when I run away," said Josie. "I may as well leave tonight."

But just as she spoke, the shed door opened. It was Frakin.

6

The Accident

*F*oolin' about, are ya?" said Frakin.
"Come along." He grabbed Daniel by the
arm. "Yer brother," he said to the princess,
"he's been in an accident."

Josie almost dropped Elvis. She had
been holding him behind her back.

Ozzie? In an accident? She had wished
he would fall off his horse, but she didn't
really want him to break his neck. Even

if he did pretend to be perfect.

"Is he hurt?" she asked Frakin.

"Sprained his arm only," said Frakin. "It's his mare what's suffrin' most." He started down the path to the stable.

Josie dropped Elvis into the basket beside his mother. She shut the shed door. Then she ran along behind Frakin to see Ozzie's horse.

Blue lay on her side on a blanket on the hay. She was moaning. Her leg was wrapped in wet cloths. Her eyes were half closed.

"Blue's bruised her foreleg," said Frakin. "It were a bad fall."

"Can't we help her?" asked Josie. She could not stand the sound Blue was making.

"Someone 'as to stay with her," said
Frakin, "and rinse the cloths in cool water.
But I've too many other horses as needs
tendin'."

Josie stroked Blue's mane. "I'll stay with
her," she said. "I'll take care of her."

Josie sat down beside Blue. She rinsed the cloths. Frakin showed her how to wrap Blue's leg. "Sing to her," said Frakin. "Animals like that."

"I know," said Josie.

She sang "The Gypsy Rover."

She sang "Camptown Races."

She sang until Blue was quiet. Then Josie lay down beside her and fell sound asleep.

"Best get on back," said Frakin. He shook the princess gently. "I'll look after Blue this night." He lit his pipe.

"Will she be all right?" asked Josie.

Frakin puffed on his pipe. Then he leaned over. But he didn't answer yes or no—he just stroked Blue's cheek.

"She's strong," he said, "and steady. But she'll need ya agin tomorra."

Josie faltered. How could she come tomorrow? She had to run away tonight. But she said, "I'll try to come."

"Good then," said Frakin. "Until tomorra."

So Josie latched the stable door. Then

she walked slowly back to the palace.

What in the world should she do? Josie wondered. What would happen to her if she stayed? What would happen to Blue if she left? What would happen to Elvis if she didn't?

There had to be someone who would take a fat black kitten. Someone who loved animals . . .

Josie thought of someone. She would ask him tomorrow. But she would pack her suitcase tonight. Just in case.

7

Too Late to Run Away

Y ou did what?" said Daniel.

"I gave Elvis to Frakin," said Josie.

Daniel's face went pale. His eyes opened wide.

"What did he say?"

"He said, 'Thank you very much,'" said Josie. "He said he hadn't had a present in a very long time. But he asked me to look after Elvis. Just for today."

She went on brushing Blue's long tail. She was getting ready to braid it.

Daniel picked up the ribbon Josie had brought to tie Blue's tail. He dangled it in front of Elvis. Elvis swiped at it with his paw. He missed.

Daniel dragged it slowly in front of the kitten. Elvis pounced on it. Then he rolled over and over until his black body was all tangled up in the blue ribbon.

"I'm glad," said Daniel. "I'm glad Elvis is going to stay."

Josie finished braiding Blue's tail. She untangled Elvis from the ribbon. Then she tied a neat bow on the end of Blue's tail.

"There!" she said. "Now she'll look beautiful when Ozzie comes to see her."

Prince Osbert was feeling better. His

right arm was in a sling. He petted Blue
with his left hand and rubbed his nose
against hers.

"Beauty," he whispered.

Then he sat with Josie all day long while
she and Elvis sang songs to Blue and
wrapped and rewrapped her leg.

"Where in heaven's name have you
been?" asked Nanny when Josie came in.
"And in such a state!"

"Better late than never," Josie said. That's
what Nanny herself always said. But Nanny
didn't seem to hear.

"Missed your lunch . . . late for tea . . .
the queen and king . . . both in a state . . .
letter from the library . . . brush this hair . . .
nice clean dress . . . now off with you!" She
shoved Josie out the door.

The princess sighed. So the library notice had finally come. It was too late to run away.

She walked along the grand hall to the royal dining room. Her heels echoed on the marble floor. Shiny suits of armor stood guard all along the grand hall. Silently they said, "You can't sneak away now."

Josie walked by them, one by one. The last one next to the huge door held an ax overhead. The princess looked up at it. She shuddered. But then she took the big handle of the dining room door and pulled it open.

8

Telling the Truth at Tea

Queen Cristobel sat at the end of the long table. Silver trays of tiny sandwiches and cakes were set on the white linen. Josie smelled hot scones. She saw a cut-glass bowl of shiny red strawberries and cream.

But even though she had forgotten lunch she did not feel hungry. She sat down in her place across from Ozzie and waited.

"Josephina," her mother began, "a letter
has come from the library."

Josie looked down at her plate. She
didn't say anything. The queen went on.

"A book about dog care was checked out

to me. It is now overdue. Do you know anything about this?"

"I took it out," Josie admitted. "I wanted to learn about dogs. To prove I could take care of one."

"Where is the book now?" asked King Max.

"I wrecked it," said Josie. "I left it out in the rain. Then I tried to get money to pay for it. But I couldn't."

She looked down again. There was nothing else to say.

"Josephina," said the queen, "I am sorry about the book. But I am glad you told us the truth."

King Max was silent. Then he said, "I think that you should take care of Blue until Ozzie's arm is better. To learn a lesson about caring for things."

"But she's already taking care of Blue," said Ozzie. "Since yesterday!"

"So we understand," said the queen. "Frakin told us that Josie was doing a good job. And that she nursed a weak kitten back to health, all by herself."

"You have proved that you can look after animals," said King Max. "So your mother and I have decided that you may have a dog for your birthday. Any dog you like."

Josie couldn't believe it—her prayer had been answered after all. She could get a dog! Any dog she wanted. But then she thought of Blue . . . her big eyes . . . her long, silky tail . . . her gentle beauty.

"Thank you," said Josie, "but I think I'd like a horse better. You see, I love horses more than anything else in the whole world!"

Then she remembered Elvis. "Except for cats, of course," she said.

King Max looked at Queen Cristobel. The queen started to laugh. The king did, too.

"Josephina," he said, "you can have anything. Absolutely anything your heart desires."

Josie smiled. In that case, she would have a puppy, too. Suddenly she felt very hungry. She ate three sandwiches. She ate two pieces of cake. She ate one bowl of strawberries. Then she licked the whipped cream off her fingers and closed her eyes.

She imagined her eighth birthday party. She would give all the children rides on her beautiful white horse.

She would let them take turns playing with her new puppy.

And when it was time to blow out the candles on her cake, Elvis would sing.

Enjoy More Hyperion Chapter Books!

ALISON'S PUPPY

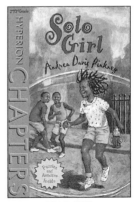

SPY IN THE SKY

SOLO GIRL

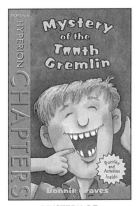

**MYSTERY OF
THE TOOTH GREMLIN**

**MY SISTER
THE SAUSAGE ROLL**

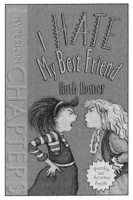

I HATE MY BEST FRIEND

**ALISON'S FIERCE AND
UGLY HALLOWEEN**

SECONDHAND STAR

GRACE THE PIRATE

Hyperion Chapters

2nd Grade
Alison's Fierce and Ugly Halloween
Alison's Puppy
Alison's Wings
The Banana Split from Outer Space
Edwin and Emily
Emily at School
The Peanut Butter Gang
Scaredy Dog
Sweets & Treats: Dessert Poems

2nd/3rd Grade
The Best, Worst Day
I Hate My Best Friend
Jenius: The Amazing Guinea Pig
Jennifer, Too
The Missing Fossil Mystery
Mystery of the Tooth Gremlin
No Copycats Allowed!
No Room for Francie
Pony Trouble
Princess Josie's Pets
Secondhand Star
Solo Girl
Spoiled Rotten

3rd Grade
Behind the Couch
Christopher Davis's Best Year Yet
Eat!
Grace the Pirate
The Kwanzaa Contest
The Lighthouse Mermaid
Mamá's Birthday Surprise
My Sister the Sausage Roll
Racetrack Robbery
Spy in the Sky
Third Grade Bullies